THE HORSE NEXT DOOR

LINDA HANCHEY

Cushing Publishing
www.cushingpublishing.com

Copyright 2024 Linda Hanchey
ISBN 978-1-963661-06-4

Cushing Publishing
P.O. Box 38
Middlesex, NC 27557

Table of Contents

Prologue

"Mom, did you see anything?" I leaned over her shoulder to get a better look. We had been under this big oak tree for several hours. She was so good to come with me repeatedly to look for Blue Boy. "I just know he is running with the wild horses. He would be with them if we could find the wild ones."

Mom handed me the binoculars and started to stand. "Raven, you might be right, but we aren't seeing anything today, so let's pack things up and move on. The café should still be open. I sure could use a cup of coffee."

It was hard for her to understand that I didn't care how late it was. I didn't want to eat. I wanted to stay right here and keep looking for Blue Boy. I'd heard the wild ones had been seen on that ridge occasionally. I pulled myself up and began walking towards the truck. If only Blue Boy would come back. I didn't understand why he would leave. I thought at one time maybe someone had stolen him, but how could they ever catch him? He was so wild. Then I thought maybe he went to join the wild herd. They may be part of his family. He could be anywhere. We were sitting in the Appalachian Mountain Range. The mountains went on forever. I wished I knew he was safe. I missed him. He was my buddy. I would have run away if it weren't for him. We had just moved here from the city. I hadn't wanted to move. I missed my old life, my friends, my house. When we moved to the mountains, I thought my life was over. Then I found Blue Boy, or maybe he found me.

One day, while walking to the bottom of the hill surrounding our house, I saw, on the ridge in the distance, a horse running at full speed. His feet hardly touched the ground. I thought I was dreaming. Then I watched him disappear over the rise. I couldn't believe it. In the pasture, our next-door neighbor had the most beautiful horse I'd ever seen. I could hardly contain myself as I ran to tell Mom. A

7

horse right here. My dreams were coming true. It then occurred to me that maybe living here wouldn't be so bad.

I went to look for him every day. Every day, he would appear, getting closer and closer. Over time, we became best friends. I never missed a day going to see him, and he never missed a day being there. Until one day he was gone.

The Farm

According to Mom, I've always been horse crazy. She said I had a stuffed pink pony I took with me everywhere. I slept with it; I ate with it. The fact is, I still have "Horsey." Not as pink, missing one ear, stuffing about gone, but right beside my pillow every night. I think loving horses is something you are born with. My mom and dad didn't show any interest in them. We lived in the city. They liked the city life. They took me on pony rides and bought me books. I had horse pictures all over my walls. I couldn't get enough of horses.

When I was young, still in elementary school, my dad died. My dad and I were best friends. I can remember him riding me on his shoulders and us both laughing. I can remember playing tag with him. Hide and seek was my favorite. He wasn't good at hiding; I found him every time. We would go to the park. He would swing me so high that Mom would yell. That made him go even higher, and we would really laugh then. Sometimes, he would sneak me a piece of candy and tell me not to let Mom know. We would laugh. I sure did miss him.

My dad was a Marine stationed in North Carolina when they found out that he had cancer. Not long after that, he died. I don't know if I completely understood things about illness or a person dying. Mom told me he had gone to heaven and was now watching over us from there. I couldn't believe he would leave us. Mom told me God needed him more. She said she was mad at God. I think I was, too.

The next several months were a blur. I didn't remember much other than hearing Mom crying late at night. Then one evening, she came into my room and told me we were moving. Her face was so sad, and tears fell as she said, "Raven, we are moving to the mountains."

I yelled. I couldn't believe what she was saying. I wasn't moving.

THE HORSE NEXT DOOR

I had friends here. I liked my house. I liked my room. "Mom, I am not moving."

"Raven, since the passing of your father, I have been doing everything I could to hold on to our place here. I tried. I cannot afford to stay. Your father would understand. We are moving to the farm he inherited. It's in Virginia, in the Blue Ridge Mountains. It's so beautiful there. There are the cutest houses and lots of land. We may be able to get you a horse one day. Think of that, your very own horse."

I couldn't hear a word she said because I wasn't going to move, period. She continued trying to convince me it was for the best. She said I'd make new friends. We would be happy there. My thoughts were about how and why this was happening. *My life is ruined*, I thought. *I may have to go, but I'm going to hate it. What choice do I have? I'm just a kid.*

The next day, she sat me down again. I was calmer. I guess the news had finally set in. She told me about my dad and why he had a farm in the mountains. First, she told me how they met. Her best friend had set them up on a date. They hit it off right away, and a year later, they were married. She said after they married, they would visit his parents, who lived on this mountain farm. This was a family farm that had been handed down through several generations. On one of Mom and Dad's visits, Dad's parents surprised them by saying they were moving to Florida. The winters were getting too harsh for their old bones; warmer climates in Florida would be much more pleasant. They then announced they were giving the farm to Dad. It came as a real surprise to both of them.

She explained that the land had been in the family since the early 1900s. His great-grandparents had homesteaded 260 acres, something the government did to help people by giving them land to work. And they did. They struggled through the years to make a fine farm for their family. They raised their children, teaching them how to be self-sufficient. They learned to hunt, to plant, to preserve. They built their two-room house out of locust wood harvested from the property. They had no electricity. A nearby creek provided water for themselves and their livestock. They raised hogs, cows, and chickens. It was a good life. When the children were of age, they all left the mountain looking for jobs. My grandfather joined the Marines. He soon got married, and they had one son, my dad. After years of being away from the mountain, my grandfather built a better house for his parents. That is the house we would be moving to. Mom said it was a pretty house. All I could think was, *Great, we are moving into a house without running water and electricity. I'm going to be a regular hillbilly.* I guess Mom saw the look on my face. She looked at me and said, "Yes, it now has heat, running water, and electricity." We both laughed. Not long after the house was built, my grandparents moved back to the farm to care for their parents. That is where my dad lived as a young boy. He grew up playing in those mountains.

Mom also told me a caretaker was living in the old home place. His name was Mr. Jim. He had been given lifetime rights to live on the property. Mom said she had met him, and he was nice. She said he grew up in these mountains and would help us on the farm.

Mom sat beside me, looking off into the distance worriedly. Then she said, "We are going to be fine. Your dad will be watching over us. We will learn to love the mountain as much as we love it here."

Several weeks later, we were packed and ready to go. Our neighbors came by to wish us well and promised they would come to visit. I wasn't sure if they would. I just knew I didn't want to leave my home. Everything was changing. Everything had changed.

The ride was long. I didn't think we would ever get there. This was my first time in the mountains, or at least the first time I could remember. The mountains sure were big. The roads were so crooked I almost got car sick. Then Mom announced, "We're here. Look, there is our new house, up on the hill." I hated to admit it, but it was really pretty surrounded by all those mountains.

We turned up the long drive. There on the porch was an older man. Mom said it was Mr. Jim. He stood up, walked to our car, and opened Mom's door. "Hi, ladies," he said with a great big smile. "Hope your journey was pleasant. I've put a pot of coffee on the stove. You must be Raven." He looked over at me and gave me a wink. I thought I was going to like him. "Young lady, I have some fresh milk for you." He helped bring in our luggage. We didn't bring a whole lot of anything but our clothes and some personal items. The house was like when Dad's parents lived there, full of furniture, old pictures on the wall, and knickknacks everywhere. Mom showed me my room. It smelled like old people and had ugly flower wallpaper. I didn't know if I could do this. Mom read my mind. She said, "Honey, we will paint it any color you like. It will be fine when you get your horse pictures up." All I could think of was how much I already missed my old house. I didn't know how this was going to work.

After we finished bringing everything in, we sat on the big wrap-around porch. The view was incredible. Mom sat with her coffee and talked to Mr. Jim about things they would look at around the farm tomorrow. I got a glass of milk, leaned against the wall, and tried to find a positive thought. That would take some doing.

The next several days went by quickly. We were unpacking, cleaning, and rearranging furniture. The neighbors came to bring home-cooked goodies, cookies, and cakes. Some brought fresh vegetables and homemade biscuits. Everyone seemed nice. I especially liked the girl who came with the lady who made biscuits. The girl's name was Annie; I think she was about my age. She said if I would like, she would introduce me to kids at school. I was glad because I was nervous about starting at a new school. Before she and her mom left, she said if I wanted, she would come back over. I told her that I would like that. I thought, *I have a new friend.*

The next day turned out to be exciting. One of our neighbors brought us chickens. Yes, chickens. The only chickens I had ever seen were from KFC and fried. No, these were real chickens. He brought us a dozen full-grown chickens. Thank goodness Mr. Jim was there to help us. He said they were laying hens and would provide us with many fresh eggs. We walked down to an older barn. "This is the chicken coop. There have been chickens on this farm as long as I can remember," he said as he took each chicken and put her in the pen. "Up there are the laying boxes. They will lay their eggs there. You must gather them daily, but always check for snakes before reaching in." He grinned as he told us this. He went on to tell us that we should turn them out of the pen after a couple of weeks but be sure to lock them up at night to keep the coyotes, hawks, and possums from eating them. My head was spinning. Snakes, coyotes, possums—*What am I doing here?* Snakes. I was supposed to put my hand under that chicken and get an egg with the possibility of a snake being there first? Nope, not doing it. I must have looked ready to faint when he said, "Always move the hen off the nest, then look to see if there is a snake. Most of the snakes are harmless and good to keep around the barn. We want them here. They eat mice." Oh, great, that made my day. Now we had chickens and welcomed good snakes. *Good snakes?*

For the next few days, we stayed busy. People from the church came by and invited us to Sunday service. I wasn't sure Mom would go since she was mad at God, but I wanted to go. Maybe there would be more kids my age there. I told Mom I wanted to go. At first, she said she didn't know if she would, but then she said yes.

It was a little white church set back in a cove. It wasn't far from our house. I learned from some of the older people that my grandparents and my dad went there. They said my dad was a very polite young boy. One lady took me over to one of the stained-glass windows. Inscribed at the bottom were my grandparents' names. The whole church was full of stained-glass windows that people had donated. A lady up front played the piano. It was a charming place. The preacher talked about forgiveness. I looked at Mom; she was wiping her eyes. I guessed she spoke with God. I wasn't sure if I was ready to talk to God. I especially missed my dad. Maybe in time, God and I would have a conversation.

After we got settled in, Mom agreed to walk with me around the farm. It was beautiful, with huge trees, big fields, and breathtaking views. The mountains didn't seem real—they were so enormous. We saw Mr. Jim and went over to talk to him. He told us the names of all the ridges and mountains. Each had a name. One was Big Sky Mountain, one was Buck Mountain, and another was Flat Ridge. He told us most of them were part of the Appalachian Trail System. He said there was a ranger station on Big Sky where we could get a map and more information. Mom and I talked and agreed to get a map and walk part of the Appalachian Trail one day. Mr. Jim continued telling us about the different paths on our farm. He said there were paths made by wildlife leading to the creek on the far side of the farm over the ridge. I thought they would be so much fun to explore.

Several days later, Mom and I went to the ranger station. We learned that you need to register if you are going into the forest or walking the Appalachian Trail. The purpose was that, if you were late coming in, they would send people out to look for you. The ranger said it was essential to stay on marked trails. He also said not to feed any wildlife, to have bear spray, and to keep hydrated.

Now, with our map, we could study the trail. We were both surprised to learn the Appalachian Trail System, which went through Big Sky Mountain along with many more mountains, was over two thousand miles long, covering thirteen or fourteen states. It would take months to cover the whole thing; you would need to be fit and do lots of planning to take that journey. Mom and I decided Big Sky would do just fine for our adventures.

If Mom couldn't take me over to the big mountain, I would explore the trails on the farm. I liked taking the paths deep into the woods and down to the creek. One time, I walked to the far side of our property. It was a pretty good way from the house. Following a path through the woods, I came out to this field. At the bottom of the field, I came to a fence.

That's when I saw him. The most beautiful horse I'd ever seen running across the ridge. I was in awe, watching him move as if the wind carried him. His coat glistened in the sun. He was so black he looked blue. His mane tossed around like feathers. When he reached the higher ridge, he stopped, reared up, shook his head, and stood motionless like a king overlooking his kingdom. He stood like that for the longest time, took one leap, and was gone. I stood there, frozen. I couldn't move. I felt I'd seen something out of a dream. I just saw the most magnificent horse. Then I realized this beautiful horse was in my neighbor's pasture. I couldn't wait to tell Mom about the horse next door.

The Horse Next Door

I ran as fast as I could to the house. Running in through the kitchen, I yelled, "Mom, Mom, I found a horse! A real one, living in our neighbor's field! He is the most beautiful horse I've ever seen!"

"Slow down, Raven. You found a horse? Where? Where have you been?"

"He was at the back side of our farm! There's a fence! He was in there!"

"Did you climb the fence? You had better not. You don't go on other people's property without permission. Anyway, how do you know if that horse is mean or not? Don't go over there, do you hear me?"

"But Mom, you don't understand!" I pleaded with her.

"Raven, I understand enough, and you best hear me. Don't go over that fence. Is that clear?"

"But Mom, what about the horse? We've got to find out more about him. There is a horse next door, can you believe it?" I was so excited that I couldn't help but picture myself riding across that ridge with my hair flying, running as fast as the wind.

"Raven, I will ask about the horse if you will be patient and promise me you won't climb that fence. I will ask around about the horse, and we can go from there. Okay?"

I nodded while dreaming of our ride together, me and the horse next door.

I couldn't sleep that night; I could only think of that beautiful horse. I imagined myself riding him up and down the mountains, just me and this magnificent horse. Hopefully, Mom would talk to Mr. Jim tomorrow to see who owned that pasture below us. I knew in the morning I'd be going back down there. I wondered if he liked apples. I went to the kitchen to see if we had any.

"Raven, what are you doing up?"

THE HORSE NEXT DOOR

"I want to see if we have any apples so I can feed the horse," I told her as I looked for them.

"Go to bed. It's getting late. You can do that in the morning."

"Mom, we don't have any apples or carrots. Can we go to the store in the morning?" I asked as I headed back to my room.

"Yes, we will go in the morning. Now good night for the third time." I could tell she was smiling when she sent me to my room. *Good*, I thought, *tomorrow we will get treats.*

We went to the store first thing. Mom was shopping for other stuff. I picked up a whole bag of fresh apples and a bunch of carrots. I told her I didn't want to run out. She laughed and said not to feed them all at once. I thought that if that horse wanted ten apples, he would get ten.

When we got home and put the groceries away, Mom and I walked out to find Mr. Jim to ask him about the person who owned the field adjoining ours. Mr. Jim was pulling weeds in the garden. Mom said as we approached that we should be helping him. I thought, *Not today; I have a horse to see.*

Mr. Jim stopped and greeted us. I began telling him about the horse I saw the day before. Mom expressed concern, saying she wanted to meet the owner before letting me near him. Mr. Jim didn't know anything about a horse. He said he never went down to that part of the farm. He did tell us the pasture belonged to a man named Mr. Barnhill. He said he was a retired veteran, not from around these parts. He also said that he wasn't very welcoming. Some of the church people tried to bring him food and be neighborly. When they went to his house, he said he didn't want any food and for them not to come back and bother him. Mr. Jim said he never left the house. He even has his food delivered. A boy from the grocery store drops food off twice a month. He said the boy complained to his boss that Mr. Barnhill never left a tip. The boss told him that this man fought for our country's freedom and that it was our duty to serve him. So the boy had to deliver and not get a tip. Mom asked Mr. Jim if he thought it would be okay for us to go over there. Mr. Jim just shrugged his shoulders. Then Mom volunteered me to help pull weeds. Mr. Jim said he would appreciate the company. The last thing I wanted to do to was pull weeds. I had a horse to see.

"Mr. Jim, do you think that man will let me ride his horse?" I asked.

Mr. Jim said, "I don't know. I didn't know he even had one. Most likely, he is wild, so be careful. You do know there are wild horses. They have been seen all over these mountains."

"Really? Are they on Big Sky Mountain?" I asked.

"People have seen them on Big Sky, Buck Mountain, Eagle's Nest Mountain, throughout both Virginia and North Carolina," he responded.

Now I was even more excited, horses everywhere. I thought, *I'm going to like living here after all.* We continued to pull weeds, and his talking about knowing my father when he was a boy made pulling a much more pleasant task. I loved hearing about my dad, and I sure missed him. I wished I could tell him about the horse next door and the wild ones on these mountains. I decided I'd ask God to tell my dad when I prayed tonight.

Mom promised she would go over to the neighbor's that afternoon, but first, she had to bake some banana bread to take to the lady from church who just got home from the hospital. She said she would make one to give to the neighbor, too. I was excited to go with her, but she told me I couldn't. I was so disappointed. She said, "I bet you will make your bed from now on like you should. If you had this morning, you could have gone. So go up and make your bed. I'll be back soon." I forgot to make my bed in all the excitement over the horse. I bet I would from now on. I wondered if he would tell Mom the horse's name.

I heard the back door open. I ran to find out what the man said. When she came in, she looked so flustered. "Mom, what did he say? Did he tell you the horse's name?" I pleaded for answers.

Mom replied sternly, "You are never to go over there. That was the rudest man I've ever met." She then told me that she knocked on the door several times. She was about to leave when the door opened, and there stood an older, unkempt man. He said, "What do you want?" Mom told him we had just moved in and that she had come by to introduce herself and bring him some banana bread. He told her, "I don't need any food!" Then he slammed the door in her face.

THE HORSE NEXT DOOR

That was it. How was I supposed to find out about this horse if he wouldn't even talk to my mom? *What am I going to do now?* I asked myself. Sometimes life didn't make sense. I knew what I was going to do. I was still going to take apples to this horse. I would also name him. Maybe it wouldn't be his real name, but it would be for me.

Mom said I could go to the fence but not over it. I got up at daybreak the following morning. I also made my bed. I grabbed my backpack, went to the kitchen, and filled it with apples and carrots. Today was going to be a good day. I headed to the back field, hoping he might be there. He wasn't. So I sat, waiting. After several hours of not seeing him, I decided to leave and return later. But first, I rolled several apples under the fence, hoping he would smell them and come back across the ridge. I returned that afternoon; the apples were still there, and there was no horse. Maybe he would come tomorrow.

Starting that day and every day after, I would go and sit by the fence. Sometimes, the apples would still be there; sometimes, I could tell they had been bitten. I figured it must have been a squirrel or deer that left its mark—still no signs of a horse.

Then one day, I saw him. He was up on the ridge. I stood next to the fence. I rolled some fresh apples under, hoping he would come. Then, without warning, he came thundering down the hill, running at full speed right towards me. He scared me something awful. I backed away. It looked like he was going to come right through the fence. Then he came to a sliding stop, tossed his head, grabbed an apple, and was gone. I hardly had time to take a breath, it happened that fast. I stood there trembling. I didn't know if it was from fear or pure excitement. He was even more beautiful than I could have imagined. He had a thick sweeping mane, big muscles, and a long, arched neck. His coat was blue-black with white hair running throughout like a blue heeler dog. I'd never seen that color on a horse before. It was unique. This was the most exciting thing I'd ever experienced. This felt like a dream.

From that day forward, I would return to the fence, roll an apple under it, and wait. He came back. Each day, he would come charging down. I got braver and would stand up at the fence, trying not to back off when he charged. One day, he stopped at the fence, and instead of immediately running off, he stood. I got up my nerve, picked up an apple, and reached over the fence. He tossed his head and flared his nostrils. Then, with the most tender mouth, he took the apple from me. I slowly reached for another apple and handed it to him. He gently took it. I never imagined I would be standing next to such a magnificent horse. I loved him so much.

Each day, I would go at the same time. Several times, he would already be standing at the fence. We both seemed to be more relaxed with each other. He wasn't running away, and I wasn't scared. Then one day, after he had taken an apple from me, I touched him. He didn't move. I began to rub his neck. This was the most beautiful feeling I'd ever had. He stood there as I ran my fingers over his coat. I touched his face, and he closed his eyes. I couldn't explain it, but I knew he loved me too. That was when his name came to me: Blue Boy. His name would be Blue Boy.

Each day, I believed we became closer to each other. I didn't tell Mom, but I did go under the fence. I spent hours with him, talking to him and brushing him. He would just stand there. Sometimes he would reach around and smell my hair. Sometimes he would nuzzle my shoulder. I had never felt such love as we shared every day.

Then my worst nightmare began. When I got to the fence, he wasn't there. I waited and waited. I called him. I sat and waited. I climbed under the fence and made my way to the top of the ridge, calling his name. He didn't show. Where was he? For the last several weeks, he had been there every day. Something must have happened. Blue Boy was gone.

I ran home as fast as I could, bursting into the house, crying, "Mom, Blue Boy is gone! He wasn't there in the field! He didn't come when I called! Something bad has happened!"

Mom took me by the shoulders. "What's going on? Settle down and talk slower. What happened?"

Between tears, I tried to tell her that Blue Boy was missing. Something had to be wrong for him not to come to me. She tried to assure me that Blue Boy was okay. He will show up in a day or so. She told me to be patient. He was all right. I wanted so much to believe her, but in my heart, I knew something was wrong. Blue

Boy would never leave me. He just wouldn't. I finally went upstairs, threw myself across my bed, and cried. The last time I had cried like this was when my daddy died. This felt about the same. I loved Blue Boy, and I knew he loved me.

The following day, Mom said she would ask Mr. Jim if he had seen Blue Boy, and also have him ask at the store if anyone in the neighborhood had seen him. I hardly slept that night and couldn't wait for daybreak. When the sun finally came up, I took off. I just knew Blue Boy would be there waiting. But when I got down the hill, I saw he wasn't there. My heart sank. I slipped under the fence and ran to the top of the ridge to get a better look. I could see all around, through fields and across hills. He wasn't anywhere to be seen. I stood there for the longest time, just wanting to see him, even if he was far off. He wasn't. I fell to the ground and cried.

On my way home, I thought maybe there was a hole in the fence that he may have gone through, so I followed the fence line along the woods. The fence wasn't down anywhere I could see. I looked for tracks—no signs of a horse. I went down to the creek and looked for tracks down there. Nothing. There was only one thing left to do, and that was to go see Mr. Barnhill.

I ran as fast as I could across the field, climbed through the fence, and headed towards his back door. I knew Mom would be furious, but this was an emergency. The yard was overgrown with tall grass and weeds. I had to make a path. I stepped up on the stoop and knocked. No one came to the door. I knocked again louder. When no one answered, I headed to the front door. The front yard was no better than the back, with grass up to my knees. The car was in the driveway; it didn't look like it had been moved in a while. Newspapers were lying on the ground around the mailbox. I knocked on the front door. I wasn't sure how he would react to me telling him that his horse had gone missing. I hoped he wouldn't blame me. I knocked again. Still no one came to the door. I gathered enough courage to look through the window. The place was messy: there were papers everywhere and dirty plates on the coffee table. I could see into the kitchen, and the sink was overflowing with dishes. Something didn't look right. I knocked again and yelled his name. Still no response. I needed to tell Mom. I sprinted through the overgrown yard, climbed the fence, and returned home.

Opening the back door, I called, "Mom!" She came in from the living room.

"Raven, why in the world are you so out of breath?" Mom asked with concern.

"Mom, something isn't right with Mr. Barnhill."

She looked at me. "What, you have been to Mr. Barnhill's after I told you not to go over there? What has gotten into you?"

"Listen, I'm sorry, but I just had to know if he took Blue Boy away or to let him know his horse may be hurt. I'm sorry." Mom was so mad I was almost afraid to continue, but I did. "When I knocked on his back door and no one came, I went to the front door. The yard was so overgrown. I knocked, and still no one answered. I looked through the window. It was such a mess in there. Papers and dishes everywhere. Mom, do you think Mr. Barnhill is dead?"

"Raven!" Mom yelled. "Don't say such a thing! Maybe he hasn't felt like cleaning, and he is just sleeping. Don't you go back over there! I'll tell you what, so we both feel better, I'll call the sheriff and ask them to do a wellness check. I'm sure everything is all right." She reached over and hugged me. "I'm still mad at you for going over there after I told you not to. Don't go over there again, you hear me?"

I agreed. Then I asked, "What about the horse? Can you get the sheriff to ask about Blue Boy?"

"Let's take one thing at a time. I'm sure the horse is fine. I'm sure Mr. Barnhill is fine. You have got to stop getting so worked up over these things." Then she kissed me on the forehead and told me to go gather eggs, and she would call the sheriff. *Great, I'm having a terrible day, and now I've got to go collect eggs and watch out for snakes.* The last thing I wanted to do was to touch a snake in a chicken's nest. I wondered why snakes liked chicken eggs—I'd put my hand under a hen more than once without touching an egg, since the snakes had gotten to it first. I thought I'd rather eat dirt than collect eggs. I went reluctantly to the chicken coop. Thank goodness I found eggs and no snakes. When I got back, Mom said the sheriff would go do a wellness check and may stop by here to talk to me.

It was getting dark when the sheriff pulled up to the house.

THE HORSE NEXT DOOR

Mom invited him in. He stood at the door and told us that Mr. Barnhill no longer lived there. His son had put him in a nearby nursing home. The son said Mr. Barnhill had dementia and post-traumatic stress disorder. He said he was no longer able to take care of himself. I jumped in quickly to ask, "What about the horse? What did they do with Blue Boy?" The sheriff looked at my mom, questioning what I was asking. I said, "The horse that was in the back field behind his house, where did they take him?"

The sheriff said he did not mention a horse when he talked to the son. "I will call him again and see and let you know if I find anything." He wrote down our phone number, turned, and left. I stood there looking at Mom, wondering what they had done with Blue Boy. I had to know. *Please tell me they didn't sell him*, I begged. I began to cry, thinking they could have. I ran to my room. This couldn't be happening.

We didn't hear anything from the sheriff's office for the next few days. Mom knew I was upset. She told me we would look for Blue Boy; maybe he was still around. She told me not to think he had been sold until we heard back from the sheriff. We began walking the paths leading through the woods and around the fields. We walked the ridge, we walked the pastures, we walked along the creek. We saw no signs of a horse. I put carrots and apples out. Most of them were still there when I checked. There were only deer tracks around them. My hope was dwindling. Then I did something I hadn't done in a while. I prayed. I asked God to return Blue Boy or let me know he was all right. I added too that I hoped he hadn't taken him to heaven like he did my dad. I promised I wouldn't be mad at Him anymore if He would let me know about Blue Boy. I wasn't sure if He heard me; I had to believe He did. Sunday School taught me that God hears our prayers and wants the best for us. I believed the best would be not to take Blue Boy to heaven and to let me know he was all right.

The sheriff called Mom later that week. He told Mom he contacted the son, who said he knew nothing about horses. The son said he would talk to his dad, but he doubted if that would help since his dad didn't know him or where he was. He was in the last stages of this horrible disease, and Mr. Barnhill could hardly communicate. Still, he would ask.

We continued to look. Even Mr. Jim walked with me. We didn't find any signs of a horse anywhere. There were no broken fences. There wasn't a gate open. There were no hoof prints at the creek. How could this horse just disappear?

The Search

It had been several months since Blue Boy disappeared. We had thought of all the scenarios as to the reason for his disappearance. Could someone have stolen him when they found Mr. Barnhill had moved? Did Mr. Barnhill give him away or sell him? Mom and I even went to the nursing home to talk to him. He, of course, didn't know us. The nurse said he was nonverbal. We tried to get a response; he didn't even make eye contact. Mom and I went to the stockyard. They had a horse sale once a month. The yard owner said he hadn't seen any horse fitting Blue Boy's description. He called a few horse traders to ask them. They didn't know anything either. Mom gave them her number just in case he did show up there. Mom and I and sometimes Annie went with us to the state park and talked to the rangers. We thought they might have seen him running with the wild horses. They had not. We spoke to campers and hikers, and they all said they would contact Mom, but none had seen him. We even asked some of our church members who liked hiking about him. I kept a journal of the trails we walked. Some were on Sky High Mountain, and some were on Deer Mountain. The creek kept us from going over to Buck Mountain. I wanted to keep track of where we had been. Of course, when we heard the wild horses had been seen, we would go to where they were. We still had no luck finding Blue Boy.

On the fifth Sunday of the month, our church family had a gathering where we all got together and had a meal at someone's house. Everybody brought food. It was our time to host. We set up tables. Mr. Jim had the fire pit going; everyone brought chairs. There was so much food: fried chicken, string beans, potato soup, potato salad, deviled eggs, ham, collards, corn—I couldn't even name it all, there was so much. These mountain people knew how to cook. The best desserts were upside-down pineapple cake, chocolate cake, blueberry cobbler, and banana pudding, my favorite. Everyone talked and had the best time. After the meal, there were several who brought their instruments and played. I especially liked watching the old people dance; they called it flatfoot. We kids hung around the fire, making s'mores. Mr. Jim kept the fire going. He didn't go to church, but he sure enjoyed those dinners. You should have seen his plate; it was piled ten feet high.

Annie and I hung out. We had a lot in common. She loved animals too. She liked horses but was not as crazy about them as me. She understood how hard it was for me to lose Blue Boy. We spent the nights at each other's houses, sometimes talking way into the night. It was nice having a good friend to share things with. There were other kids eating s'mores, and someone brought up Blue Boy. They were intrigued when they heard about all the places we had looked. Annie's older brother Billy mentioned he had seen wild horses on the other side of the river several years ago. We girls usually didn't listen to him, but I wanted to hear more tonight. He said once he and his dad had taken the canoe downriver across to Buck Mountain. He said it was rugged. They stayed a few nights deer hunting. One morning before daybreak, they heard rustling in the woods. His dad got the shotgun out just in case it was wolves or a bear. Waiting just outside their tent, they stood motionless, waiting for whatever would break out of the woods. Then the brush opened, and a mare and foal appeared. As soon as she broke through, she saw the two of them, turned with her baby, and was gone. Billy said it happened so fast. He and his dad caught their breath, relieved it wasn't something that would eat them. Billy then started talking to some girl.

I was so excited. "Annie, did you hear that Buck Mountain has wild horses?"

Annie looked at me and said, "That was several years ago. He could have made that story up anyway. You can't believe everything he says."

"Yes, but what if it's true? What if Blue Boy is running with the wild horses over there? He could have swam across the river and joined up with them. That may be where he came from, the wild horse bunch on Buck Mountain. Annie, we have got to go over there!"

"Are you crazy? I'm not crossing that river. You aren't crossing that river. It's too dangerous." Annie was saying all this, but I wasn't listening. I had to go over there. "No, no, no! Your mom and my folks wouldn't even begin to let us go. Number one, we can't get across the river. Number two, you can't go by yourself, and I'm not going because I'm afraid of being eaten by a bear, wolf, or whatever else is over there. Number three, just plain NO!"

Annie had her opinion for sure. She was adamant we weren't going to Buck Mountain. "Listen, Annie. You and I have been camping before. We can go over there for just one night. Just enough time for me to look around. We can carry our bear spray and a .22 rifle. It'll be fun. Just think, Annie, Blue Boy could be there right now. We can do this. You MUST do this with me. You're my best pal. Please think about it. You know it would mean so much to me." I was pleading with her now.

Annie jumped in, saying, "Another thing, how do you suppose we will cross that river? Swim with tents on our backs?"

I responded quickly, "Your brother went across in a canoe. We could do that."

Then she said, "How do you suggest we get the canoe to the river? You and I don't drive."

"We can ask Billy to take the canoe for us. Only he would have to promise not to tell anyone. I know we can't tell our parents. It must be a big secret. We must make a plan. If Blue Boy is over there, I've got to go and find him." Annie nodded her head, knowing she had lost this battle. "Annie, I am still going if you don't go with me. Please, let's do this."

Annie looked at me. "Okay, on one condition: if you get hurt over there, I'm leaving you, and I won't tell anyone where you are."

I jumped up and gave her the biggest hug. "Thank you, thank you! This is going to be the best adventure ever! Now we have to talk to Billy. Do you think he will do this? Will he rat us out?"

Annie shrugged her shoulders. "I don't know. Maybe we could bribe him. We can do his homework, and if you help me, we can do his chores. It might work. I'll talk to him tonight. I think he will be in a good mood. He's over there talking to that girl, and he's smiling. We'll see. I'm not promising anything. This is the wildest thing you have ever thought about doing. Girl, we will get into so much trouble if our parents find out."

That night, I could hardly sleep, thinking about going across the river to look for Blue Boy. Now that I had convinced Annie to go, we had to get her brother on board with our plans. She said we could trust him. I hoped so. I knew if my mom found out what we were planning, she would put me on house arrest forever. Mom didn't understand the love I had for Blue Boy. I had to find him. He couldn't have just vanished. I hoped Buck Mountain would give us the answer.

With Billy possibly helping us across the river, Annie and I could manage setting up camp. We had camped on Blue Sky before. We both knew how to set up camp and get a fire going. We would be fine. I thought Blue Boy might be over there. Now that I had learned there were wild horses on that side of the river, I thought he could have joined them. Horses have a deep connection to their families; maybe that was where he came from. Instinct may have taken him home, even if he did have to swim in the river to get there. All I knew for sure was that I couldn't sleep.

Annie came the following day and had breakfast with us. We told Mom we were going hiking down to the creek. We were trying to act normal while my insides were about to bust. Through breakfast, the conversation with Mom was light. Annie kept an unreadable face. She must have known this was killing me. We helped Mom clean the kitchen, and then we headed out. I couldn't wait to get away from the house to ask. "What did he say? Will he do it?"

Annie replied, "At first, he said absolutely not. He said it was stupid and dangerous, two girls going off on a camping trip across the river. The trails have long been forgotten. He doesn't even know if any trails are usable between the rockslides and the overgrowth. He gave me a thousand reasons why we shouldn't go. Then I started bargaining with him. I told him you and I would do his homework for the rest of the year, and I think that made him change his mind. I told him I would get the phone number of the girl he was talking to at the church social. He finally agreed. He said the right thing for us to do is to tell our parents; maybe one of them would agree to go with us. The adults could set up the camp while we looked for Blue Boy. I told him they wouldn't go, and he shook his head like he knew they wouldn't."

I jumped with joy. "You're the best, Annie. Thank you so much. Are you sure he won't tell our parents? If he does, we will never see freedom again." We both laughed. We began talking about what all we needed for this trip and how to hide everything before we went. "I've got the tent. It's lightweight, big enough for two," I told her. "Can you get the sleeping bags and cooking stuff? We don't want to forget a fire starter and a good knife." We continued going over plans for the rest of the afternoon. "We can tell my mom I'm spending the night at your house, and you can tell your parents you're staying with me. We will only be gone one night, so nothing will seem different from what we usually do when we stay with each other. Will Billy haul the canoe down to the river for us? I sure hope he doesn't tell. I hope he doesn't tell his friends and someone lets it slip what we plan to do. Annie, this means so much to me. We have searched and searched this side of the river for months. Blue Boy didn't just disappear into thin air. I feel in my heart he is over on Buck Mountain."

Annie laid her hand on my arm and said, "So if we do see Blue Boy over there, then what? Have you thought about that? How are we going to explain this whole thing? Have you thought about what is going to happen to us when we tell our folks that we crossed the river by ourselves, went down a trail that may or may not exist, and spent the night where there are bears, coyotes, wolves, and let's not forget mountain lions. Do you know how much trouble we will be in? I sure hope Blue Boy is worth it."

"Annie, if I find him, it will be worth it. I'll tell your parents I made you go, that I begged and begged until you had no choice. Maybe that will help some." I gave her a reassuring smile, but I knew we would surely be in so much trouble that we would be thirty before we came off restriction.

We decided the following Saturday that we would have everything ready. Annie agreed to talk to Billy about driving us to the river with the canoe and picking us up on Sunday evening. Billy hauling the canoe in his truck wasn't anything new. He and his buddies ran the river a lot. Annie and I would put our stuff together this week and be ready to go Saturday morning.

Buck Mountain

I didn't think Saturday would ever get here. Annie and I had talked and planned all week. Billy was even involved with the last-minute details, making sure we had what we needed. We each had a backpack with water, a thermal blanket, a first aid kit, matches, a can opener, a knife, and bear spray. I was to bring the tent; she was getting the cooking stuff. We each had a sleeping bag. Once, I thought she was going to back out. It would ruin everything if she had; thank goodness she didn't. I was so worked up over this trip that I would have gone all by myself...well, maybe. Billy had agreed to bring the canoe and pick us up on Sunday. Saturday, he would leave at a different time from us so his parents wouldn't get suspicious. We were to meet him at the end of Skipper Road, which dead-ended at the river. This road wasn't used much; only locals knew about it. We planned to ride the river down to the opening Billy had told us about, where a considerable boulder stuck out over the river. There, he said we were to beach the canoe until Sunday. Then, on Sunday, take the river downstream to the state park. He said to try to be there close to five. He'd be waiting. It was all coming together. All the trouble would be worth it if we got caught. I knew I would find Blue Boy.

Saturday morning finally came. Mom didn't suspect a thing. I had taken my things out behind the old woodshed several nights before. I did have my backpack with me, which was normal when I went to stay with Annie. Mom asked if I needed a ride to her house. I told her I'd walk. It wasn't that far across the hill. I'd done it a hundred times. "See you, Mom. I'll be back Sunday evening," I said as I hugged her. Of course, as always, she told me to behave. I think that's a line all mothers use when you go out without them. Luckily for me, she was busy getting stuff ready for the church bazaar, so she wasn't paying that much attention to me. I didn't think I was showing how nervous I was, but my insides were jumping out of my skin. I was glad to leave the house as I grabbed another apple and hurried out the back door. I already had another backpack full of apples and carrots. I knew Blue Boy would come running for them. I had no doubt he was up there on Buck Mountain.

After picking up my supplies behind the woodshed, I ran to meet Annie, who was waiting for me at the shortcut to Skipper Road. She looked worried with her half smile. She said, "It's not too late to back out. We can meet Billy and tell him we changed our mind. If we get caught, you know we—"

I cut her off. "Nothing is going to happen. We are going to have a great time. We are not going to get caught. Now stop worrying. Us two girls out on our own, braving the wilderness." I chuckled. "It will be fine, and we will find Blue Boy. Just think, after all this time we have been looking, we will finally find him. Now come on, before we're late and Billy leaves us."

As we hurried along, I couldn't help but let my mind wander to Buck Mountain. I wondered how Blue Boy would look when we found him. Was he getting enough to eat? Had he been in any fights with the wild horses? Would he come to me? Did he miss me? All this was racing through my mind when Annie said, "There he is, there's Billy." He was there with the canoe as planned. That was a relief; I wasn't sure he would follow through. He didn't say a word. We unloaded the canoe and started putting our stuff in it. Billy was helping us get the last bit of gear when I saw some extra things in the canoe.

"What's all that?" I asked. He didn't respond.

Then Annie said, "Billy, what is all this?"

Billy stopped what he was doing, turned to us, and spoke. "I'm going with y'all."

Annie and I both looked at each other. "What?" we both said at the same time.

"I'm going with you two. There is no way I would let you two girls head across to Buck Mountain alone. I've been there, and it's no picnic. What kind of brother and friend would I be if I didn't go? I also went by the ranger station and gave them all the information about where we'll be and how long we'll be gone. So that's that.

Now, let's get a move on." He was firm in telling us this. I was relieved. I knew Annie was, too.

Finally, our plans were coming together as we floated downstream. *We're doing this*, I thought. *We are going to Buck Mountain.* I did feel bad not telling Mom the truth about this whole thing. I had never lied to her like this. I thought over and over how I could have done things differently. Mom saw me as a little girl. She was so protective. She didn't understand. At first, when Blue Boy disappeared, she went with me to look for him. We'd walked many miles up and down Big Sky Mountain. We'd walked all around the farm and even on Mr. Barnhill's land. We'd talked to people on the Appalachian Trail. I'd made flyers. We'd spoken to the park rangers. They even knew us by our first names, we'd been there so much. They'd promised to keep an eye out for him. But now, I thought Mom had given up. Not me; I had faith, and I prayed. I knew God wouldn't take him away from me for good. He knew the love we had for each other. Some of the kids at school had several horses. I had loved horses my whole life but never had one. Blue Boy wasn't mine, but in my heart, he was. I sure missed him. I prayed every day that God would bring him back to me. So lying to Mom might have been wrong, but I had to do this. I knew he was over there.

None of us talked as the canoe drifted down the river. We all felt the pressure knowing we had lied about this whole trip. Billy and Annie used their oars to guide us around the rocks. Then Billy pointed out the boulder. We guided the canoe to shore, pulled it out of the water, and unloaded everything. Billy had us put it behind a fallen tree so it couldn't be seen. Then he turned to us and said, "Girls, it isn't too late. We can go on further downstream. I can call a buddy, and he will pick us up. We will be grounded for years if we get caught or you get hurt." He looked straight at me. "Raven, I know this is very important to you. I wish things were different, but I'm not sure this is the right thing to do."

I looked at him with tears in my eyes. "Billy, please. I know you don't understand. I have to do this. I appreciate you two helping me and going along with this whole idea. If you decide not to go on, I'll understand. But I'm going. Blue Boy is out there. I need to find him. I need to know he is okay." Tears fell down my cheek.

Annie gave me a big hug. "Billy, we're doing this. Now come on, let's get moving."

Billy shrugged as if to say he was sorry, although I understood he just wanted to make sure we wanted to do this. We finished gathering our stuff. Billy tied the canoe and started walking. "Come on, girls, the trail is over here." We followed Billy along the shoreline, climbed over some boulders, and headed up the mountain. I was glad he came because I didn't know if we could have found this trail. It was hidden under a bunch of overgrowth. You couldn't tell that there had been a trail there. We continued moving through the weeds and brambles, and the trail became clearer. It was a beautiful day. We were all in good spirits, talking about where we would set up camp and what we would eat, and of course, I spoke of Blue Boy. The sky was beautiful against the mountains. There was a haze that made them look blue. I guessed that was why these mountains were called the Blue Ridge Mountains. I had read the Blue Ridge Mountains covered eight states. They were magnificent. The Appalachian Trail went across them and into other mountain ranges, covering thirteen or fourteen states, and was over two thousand miles long. I had walked some of the Appalachian Trail, but only a few miles up Blue Sky. One day, maybe I could do more.

We continued walking, trying to make our way. Even the deer had failed to keep the brush down. Once we reached a higher place, the mountain opened to a beautiful meadow. Billy said we would follow the edge of the woods and find a path to take us down to a creek bed. When he and his dad had come up several years before, that was how they had gone. He said a creek off the mountain would be a perfect camping spot. We continued walking. There was a much more defined trail once we reached the meadow's edge. It was clear that the deer had used this trail.

We hadn't walked far when we heard the sound of rushing water. Coming around the bend, we came upon the most beautiful creek. "Well, girls, what do you think?" Billy asked as he pointed in the direction of the water. "Just below is a small clearing. We can unpack and set up there." I couldn't have been more excited. We were here. It took a great deal of planning and, unfortunately, telling fibs. I would ask for forgiveness later. But for now, this was perfect.

Billy said he would set up camp. That way, we could go out and scout around. He gave us a general direction to head. "Follow the stream up over the rise. You will see several rock outcroppings. Stay on the creek side until you get to the top. There, you will see an opening in the trees, and from there you can see the surrounding area. Keep together, you two. Take your bear spray and this whistle. Use them if anything gets too close. Don't run. Now, if anything happens, if you see a bear, a wolf, or a snake, don't scream. Just be still. Remember, this is their territory, and we are in their home. Be careful. You have three hours. That is enough time to get your bearings, so tomorrow, when you return, you can go further. If you are not back in three hours, I am coming for you, and we will go home today. Got it?"

Annie and I both nodded as we listened to his instructions. Follow the stream. Come back in three hours. Blow the whistle if we need help. We gathered our backpacks and checked for water and bear spray. I had apples and carrots for when we found Blue Boy. Annie brought cheese and crackers and some nuts. Billy began setting up camp. Then we were off.

The Cave

The path we were on wasn't that bad. It was pretty worn, I guessed from deer. It even looked like it had been cleared at one time. We followed the stream uphill, bending around big boulders. Several trees lay across the path that we could step over. One tree was so big we had to make our way around it, losing sight of the water. It took us a bit to get back on track; there were so many rocks and dead fallen trees. We had to be quiet and listen for the river to find it again. I could now understand how easy it was to get lost. There were so many obstacles along the way to take you off the path. Annie and I continued up. Both of us were getting winded and we decided to stop. We found a level rock to sit on. The cheese and crackers hit the spot. After we rested for a short while, we headed back up again. We could see the top, which was encouraging as we were both tired of climbing.

We heard a rustling in the trees. We both stopped in our tracks and didn't move. Annie looked at me, and I looked at her as we moved closer. "What was that?" she whispered.

I shrugged my shoulders with eyes peeled toward the moving bushes. The noise continued. Annie reached for the bear spray. This was not a good place to be if a bear appeared. Staring at where the noise came from, which wasn't that far, a deer popped out. What a relief. I looked at Annie, and we both started laughing so hard we cried. "Well, I don't know when I have been so happy to see a deer," I said.

"Me either," she said, laughing. "I sure am glad we aren't bear food today." With that, we started walking back. When we reached the last boulder, we climbed to see the most beautiful meadow. Lush green grass and wildflowers were dotted throughout. There were deer grazing peacefully. Right away, I thought this would be where Blue Boy would want to go. This could be his home. I could imagine all the wild horses grazing here, the colts running around their mommas, stallions standing above, watching over their herds, defending them if needed. What a wonderful place. I was in awe. I looked at Annie; she felt the same way. We grinned at each other and gave each other a big hug. "Raven, I do believe we have found it. I think this is where we will find Blue Boy," she said.

We sat for the longest time in silence. Annie asked, "Do you want to walk the perimeter and look for tracks?" She was eager now, and I was too.

We both started walking. But first, I took a red bandana out of my backpack and hung it on a branch. "We may need to have this here to find the trail. Once we leave this spot, I want to be sure we can find our way back. Things look so different when you move around on the mountain. It's easy to get turned around and lost."

Walking along the edge of the woods, we could see where there was a worn path mostly made by animals. I didn't see any horse tracks, which was disappointing, but that didn't mean they weren't there. We walked a bit further, glancing back to keep the red scarf in view. One of the rocks was big. I asked Annie to hold my backpack so I could climb up on it to get a better look. Then I saw something. "I think I see a cave. Come on up and look," I called down to her.

Annie hollered, "Don't you go in there! That's where mountain lions, bears, and snakes are. Plus, it's cold, dark, and damp."

She kept talking as I climbed down to get a better look. "I'm just going to go to the edge and shine my light. Throw me my flashlight, will you?"

"You shouldn't go down there. You'd better not go in. Here," she said as she tossed my flashlight up to me.

"I'll be careful. I won't go in; I'm just looking from the outside." I climbed down. The cave opening was huge. "Annie, this cave is so big, you wouldn't believe it," I shouted to her. I cautiously entered the cave, shining my light along the walls. I could hear Annie telling me to be careful and not to go in, but I kept going. It was dark and damp, but I couldn't stop. I thought I saw a little light shining off in the distance. I was far enough in that I couldn't hear Annie anymore, though I was sure she was still talking. My light followed the wall. Then I saw some markings on the rock. They were drawings of some sort, like our teacher had shown us in class. Old drawings.

I hollered for Annie to see what I'd found. She didn't respond. I doubted she could hear me, and she wouldn't have come in anyway. I continued slowly. There were several types of symbols and animals, including birds, deer, and bears, but I stopped when I saw the drawings of horses. There were horses here. I knew it. Horses.

I kept moving toward the light. As I got closer, I could tell there was an opening. A big opening. I should have turned back and told Annie, but I couldn't; I had to see what was on the other side. Then I heard the sound of rushing water, getting louder. As I walked closer to the opening, I realized it was a waterfall. It fell about ten feet, and there was a path behind it leading out. I thought again about calling Annie. I couldn't stop; I had to see what was beyond the waterfall. Blue Boy could be just on the other side.

The spray from the water hit my face as I followed the well-traveled path from behind the waterfall. I made my way around the edge of the rock, careful not to slip. The roar was tremendous. I was getting wet. I shielded my eyes till I came around the side of the falls. When I lifted my gaze, I couldn't grasp what I saw. It left me speechless.

Down below in the valley were people. I rubbed my eyes, thinking I wasn't seeing right. I moved slowly on the ledge, glancing in all directions. How could this be? I was looking at a village. No one had ever mentioned that there could be *people* on this side of Buck Mountain. Even when all of us would gather around the campfires, and they would tell mountain stories, no one ever said anything about something like this. These people were completely isolated from civilization. They were so remote.

Just then, it occurred to me that they could be dangerous. Maybe they were remote for a reason. I ducked behind a big rock. I didn't know what to do. Should I get Annie? Could I run back to camp and tell Billy? Three would be better than one if there was danger. Then again, these people could be friendly. They may know something about Blue Boy.

No, I was going down there. I told myself to be brave and ready to run if I had to. There was a clear path leading downward.

I stepped slowly so as not to disturb the rocks, staying hidden till I got to the bottom. Then I had to step out into the open. I could see much better from here. Children were playing along the creek bed. There were adults moving about. They were dressed differently than I had ever seen. It appeared they were wearing traditional Native American clothing, like in the history books. My teacher had shown us movies about different Native American tribes. She'd said they had been here way before us. I couldn't imagine there were still people dressed like that. I was so mesmerized that I tripped on a branch and fell. I quickly jumped up, only to see the children running away. I wanted to say I was sorry. But when I looked up, two men were approaching me. I didn't know whether I should stay or run. I froze. I sure hoped they were friendly.

When they were close, I lifted my arm to say hi. They didn't respond but continued toward me. My heart was racing. I stepped backward, tripped on that same tree limb, and fell. One of the men rushed over and reached down to help me. He had long hair and was dressed in some animal skin. He smiled and said, "Are you okay?" He helped me stand. I shook myself off and smiled back at him. He spoke English just like me.

"I'm good. Thank you. I didn't mean to scare the children," I responded. They gestured it was okay. "I'm here looking for my horse. He isn't my horse, but I think of him as mine. He belongs to my neighbor who is in the nursing home with dementia and can't tell me where Blue Boy is because he is nonverbal." I was so nervous that I couldn't get out everything I wanted to say. It was all coming out jumbled. They looked confused and invited me into camp.

"Come, sit. We can talk here," one of the men said and began walking toward the camp. He pointed to a group of women sitting about. The ladies were all busy doing different things. We sat. One of the men looked at me and said, "Now you want to tell us about this horse? Are you by yourself?"

I replied, "No sir, Annie is waiting for me on the other side of the cave, and Billy has set up camp at the creek."

They gazed at me. I couldn't tell if they knew what I was talking about. I looked around. There were houses, not like ours, but circular structures made of grass or reeds with a roof that looked like mud. There was a hole in the middle of the roof with smoke rising out of it. The ladies near me were making some jewelry with red rocks. Another lady was braiding a blanket; another was cooking in a big pot. I couldn't help but look around in wonder. This seemed to be such a happy place. "You were telling us about a horse," the man said.

"Yes sir, Blue Boy, that's what I call him. Not just any horse. A big black horse with a long mane. He carries himself so proudly. He's my friend. We have a special bond." I looked up and noticed everyone was staring at me. "Have I said something wrong?"

One of the men spoke up. "You have met this horse you call Blue Boy?"

I responded, "Yes, sir. Blue Boy was in my neighbor's pasture. He likes apples and carrots. It took a while for us to get to know each other. We would meet every day. Then, one day, he was gone. I have looked everywhere."

"I believe you are describing one of the greatest war horses ever." He stood up. "He is known far and wide among our people. Many stories tell of his cunning, strength, and bravery. I saw him at the waterfall. Others have seen him on the ridge watching over a band of mares and foals. Our young men have tried to catch him, but like a spirit, he disappears. They try to follow him, but he is gone and leaves no trace. To catch one of his colts is the highest honor. He is a war horse, this horse you have spoken about. A hero of a horse. He is very special."

I hung on to every word. I couldn't believe what I was hearing. A real war horse. A hero horse. I asked, "How did he come to be on the other side of the river, in my neighbor's pasture?" I looked at each one of them, hoping for answers.

The man continued, "He is a spirit horse. He doesn't belong to anyone. He goes where he is needed, and when no longer needed, he returns to the mountain with his herd. You said he showed himself to you, so you must have needed him."

Bewildered, I asked, "Did he come to help me? Will he come back? Will I see him again?" I was almost in tears, realizing I might never see him again. This bond I had might have been a fleeting moment.

THE HORSE NEXT DOOR

The elderly man reached for my hand. "You are extraordinary. To have the spirit horse befriend you is something special. Treasure the times you had together. Hold his memories in your heart. If you do, he will always be with you."

I felt tears falling down my face. I didn't know why, maybe out of sadness or pure joy. I met Spirit Horse, my Blue Boy. I stood there for a moment, then I thought of the time. Oh my goodness, Annie was waiting for me on the other side of the cave. She must have been worried. Her brother had only given us three hours before he would come looking.

"I'm so sorry, I must go. Annie is waiting. Thank you all. I can't tell you what it means to hear stories about Blue Boy—I mean Spirit Horse. I will always treasure meeting you." One of the ladies walked over, cupped my hand, and placed a red stone in it, curling my hand around it. I couldn't help but hug her. Turning to leave, I wondered if I would ever see them again. For some reason, I didn't think so.

The Rescue

I began to run. I knew I had been gone too long. Annie would be calling her brother to look for me. I knew she wouldn't come into the cave by herself. When I got to the cave, everything had turned very dark. Nothing looked the same. My body felt heavy, and I couldn't open my eyes. I felt so strange. I didn't understand.

Where am I? What's going on? Why am I in this room? What are all those machines? What's in my nose? My eyes opened, trying to figure out where I was. I scanned the room. Mom was there, sleeping in a chair. *Am I in the hospital?* I asked myself. I tried to speak but only got out a groan. Mom looked up, ran over to me, and hugged me. She began to cry, rubbing my hair and cheek. "Raven, you're back! I've been so worried about you! Let me get the nurse. This is so wonderful!" She ran out of the room. I was so confused. Why was I in the hospital? I tried to remember everything. I last remembered Annie and Billy; we were on Buck Mountain. Annie and I had gone to look for Blue Boy. Billy was setting up camp. What happened?

Oh no, Mom must have known we'd crossed the river. She must have known I'd lied to her. Oh my goodness, I must have gotten hurt on the mountain. We would be in so much trouble if I did. Someone had to tell me what happened. I waited for Mom to come back into the room. I had so many questions. I also had a terrible headache. Mom came back in with the nurse. They both had huge smiles as they came to my bedside. The nurse checked the machines, and Mom just stared at me.

"Young lady, you have given us quite a scare. How do you feel?" the nurse asked politely while she was taking my pulse. I had so many questions. Mom was holding my hand, thanking Jesus out loud.

I was finally able to get the words out. "Mom, what happened? Why am I here?"

She looked at me with the sweetest eyes. "Honey, we'll talk later. You need your rest. The doctor will be in soon. We can talk about it then." She kissed me on the forehead with tears running down her face. I was tired, but I had so many questions. I closed my eyes and tried to remember anything about what happened, but my head hurt. Mom was right: I'd rest a bit.

When I woke up, I was alone in my room. I looked around, and there were flowers, stuffed animals, balloons, and cards everywhere. I wondered how long I had been here. Then I tried to reflect on the day we went to Buck Mountain. I remembered crossing the river. I remembered us getting to the creek where Billy was going to set up camp. Annie and I had headed up the mountain to look for Blue Boy. I remembered a cave that Annie wouldn't go in because she was afraid of bears, bats, and snakes. I remembered walking in. Then everything got fuzzy. Did I fall? I tried to remember more. I thought I remembered a waterfall. I didn't know.

I closed my eyes and must have drifted off again because the room was full of people when I woke up. Everyone was smiling. My mom, the preacher from church, and other church people. Annie and Billy and their mom and dad. It was like the whole community was in my room. Then they all started talking at once, saying they were so glad I woke up and was doing well. Annie looked like she had been crying for days. Her mom and dad came over, and both hugged me. The preacher laid his hand on mine and said God looked after me. Other church folks said they had been praying for me. Billy stood in the corner. I caught his eye; he gave me a smile and a wink. The preacher asked if he could pray. He thanked God for being with us young people. He asked God to give a special blessing to Billy and Annie for saving my life. When I heard that, I opened my eyes and wanted to know what he was talking about. I waited till he finished praying. The whole room said amen.

The nurse came in, seeing all the people, and said they would need to leave and that I needed to rest. With that, they either patted me on the head, kissed my forehead, or shook my hand as they left. Mom thanked them, too. It was a busy afternoon. I wanted some answers. After the last person was gone, I turned to Mom and asked, "Mom, what happened? What did the preacher mean, Billy and Annie saved my life?"

Mom replied with concern in her voice, "You fell in the cave. Annie found you. You were bleeding badly. You'd hit your head. Annie used her shirt to make a tourniquet to help stop the bleeding. She couldn't wake you, so she ran to get Billy. They knew they had to get you off the mountain for help. Billy made a gurney out of branches, sticks, and his shirt. They pulled you back down the mountain, got you to the boat, crossed the river, and called for rescue. They got you to the hospital and rushed you into surgery right away. You had lost so much blood. The doctors and nurses worked on you through the night. We didn't know if you were going to make it."

I listened and couldn't believe what I was hearing. So I had a head injury from a possible fall in the cave? Billy and Annie carried me off the mountain and saved my life? How did this happen? I closed my eyes and tried to put it all together. Why couldn't I remember? I could remember something about a waterfall, but everything was blurry.

The room gradually cleared out. It got quiet. Mom said she would get a cup of coffee and be right back. She looked so tired. I guessed she'd stayed with me the whole time. She loved me so much. Then it occurred to me that she must have known I'd lied about this past weekend. She knew I'd lied to her. Oh no. How could I have done that to her? She must have been so disappointed and upset with me. I had never lied to her before. This wasn't good. I had put her through so much. I was so sorry. I would tell her how sad I was and ask her to forgive me.

Mom came in and sat beside me. The nurse followed and added medicine to the bag hanging beside my bed. I could feel myself dozing off. I would talk to Mom about this after I got some sleep.

The next day, I started physical therapy. They helped me stand. I had a tough time getting my balance. They said it might take a while and would be hard work, but I would be running soon. Later, the doctor said I was doing great and could go home in a few days. That was good news. I couldn't wait to talk to Annie. I was worried that she and Billy had gotten into trouble over me. I wanted to apologize to them, too.

THE HORSE NEXT DOOR

I started to remember more. I wasn't clear about everything, but I did remember a waterfall. I remembered walking out from behind it. I thought I remembered a village of some sort, like a Native American village. I remembered talking to them about Blue Boy. They'd told me he was a mighty warrior. They'd called him Spirit Horse. I remembered how beautiful this place was and how friendly the people were.

I couldn't wait to tell Mom about all this, but I needed to apologize to her first. I knew I had hurt her. Someone always seemed to be coming and going in and out of my room. I would find the right time. Mom came with her knitting every day and sat with me. She brought me horse magazines and my favorite chocolate chip cookies she made. Mom said Annie and Billy wanted to come back by if I was up to it. I said of course. She called Annie's mom. "They will be here this afternoon," she said as she hung up the phone. "I'll go shopping since they are coming. I'll leave you youngsters time to yourselves. I'm sure you have a great deal to talk about." She looked at me and half-smiled. Good, I could get some answers and find out how much trouble we all were in.

They came that afternoon. Mom said she'd return after she went to the house to check on things. When the door closed, I sat up in bed and asked, "What in the world happened?"

Annie began telling me, "You went into the cave and didn't come back out. I called you over and over. You didn't answer. I went in as far as I could, but I didn't have the flashlight; you did. When I couldn't hear you, I knew something must be wrong. So I went for Billy. I hated to leave you, but I knew something terrible must have happened. It took me forever to get back to camp. I'm glad we hung that red scarf on the tree, or I would have never found my way. When I got to Billy, he was surprised you weren't with me. Then we both went into panic mode. As tired as I was, I began to pray for God to give me strength to get back to you.

"When we got to the cave, Billy ran in first. He had his flashlight and a rifle. He found you. You were unconscious, lying in a pool of blood. Billy called for me to come in. I froze when I saw you; you were so pale. He had me remove my jacket, pull the lining out, and wrap it around your head. You had a big gash that was bleeding badly. While I was doing that, he went out and started cutting tree limbs to make a gurney to get you out. We carried you out of the cave. It was such a long, hard walk back to the boat. It was getting dark. Raven, I was so scared. You weren't moving. We finally got across the river, got you in the truck, and took off, trying to get a signal. Finally, Billy was able to get 911 on the phone. They sent rescue heading toward us as we headed toward them. It wasn't long before they met us on the road. They took you. The last thing I saw was their lights headed toward the hospital. All I could do then was cry.

"We followed them to the hospital. Billy called my mom and had her call your mom. They said they would meet us there. When we got here, they had already taken you back. We waited for our parents and your mother. Your mother was hysterical because they wouldn't let her back there either. My mom called the preacher. He came and talked to your mom. The doctor came out and said you had lost a lot of blood. They were doing the best they could and would keep us posted. The preacher came and said they had started a prayer chain, and everyone was praying for you. It helped your mom to know that, and she seemed calmer. Later that night, the doctors said you were in a coma and that they would know more in the next several days. We all prayed right there in the hospital room. It was all we could do."

I could hardly believe what I was hearing. Billy looked over and said, "I think we have just been on the biggest adventure of our lives." We all started laughing. I was about to ask them how much trouble we were all in when a nurse came through the door with my supper. Billy and Annie said their goodbyes. I watched them leave and thought, *I have the best friends.*

Mom came in while I was eating. "Mom, I'm sorry. I am so sorry for lying to you. I promise I will never lie to you again." I began to cry as I watched her face. I could tell I had hurt her.

She stood up, came to me, took my hand, and said, "Yes, you did lie to me, and I am hurt and upset about that. But I'm happy to have you here safe with me. We can talk about this later. Now eat your dinner. I'm sorry, too. I should have listened. I know how much that horse means to you. As soon as you are well, we will go wherever you want and look for Blue Boy every weekend."

"Mom, listen, I know where he is," I said.

"You found him?" she questioned.

"I didn't see him but met people who told me about him."

"You met people on the mountain?"

"Yes, there was a village in the valley on the other side of the waterfall through the cave. I went through the cave and walked behind the waterfall. A wide path came out from behind it, overlooking a valley. There was a type of village below. Children were playing in the creek. Ladies were making baskets and stuff. One lady handed me a red stone when I was leaving. I hope I didn't lose it. Was it in my clothes?"

"Wait, you're saying you made it through the cave and saw a village?" She was looking at me with wide eyes.

"Yes, I did, and they told me about Blue Boy. The men told me he was a Spirit Horse, a warrior, a protector. He helps people in need. He has never been caught, but they have caught his offspring. They are cherished by these people. Mom, I knew he was special. He is a hero to these people." I continued sharing things I had seen. Mom sat down, not saying anything. She listened. She looked worried. I guessed hearing this came as a surprise. I wasn't sure by the look on her face whether she believed everything I was telling her. It was true, but maybe I could talk to her again later. Then she said I looked tired. That was her way of saying she'd heard all she could understand. So I changed the subject and finished my dinner. Mom sat and looked out the window.

Several days later, the doctors allowed me to leave. I was so glad to get out of that place. I still needed to talk with Annie and find out how much trouble she and Billy were in. The nurses came in to say goodbye. Everyone was so lovely. I could stand up and walk, thanks to physical therapy. The nurse said I had to ride down in a wheelchair, hospital policy. I was shocked when we got to the first floor and the front doors opened. Outside was a mob of people. Kids from school, more nurses, people I didn't even know, and a TV camera. Everyone was clapping. I turned to Mom. "What's going on?"

Then Annie ran up to me, followed by Billy. She gave me a big hug. Everyone was still clapping. Then a man came up to us. He was dressed in a suit. He introduced himself as the mayor. He shook my hand. Then he shook Annie and Billy's. The TV and newspaper crews had us pose for pictures. I still didn't understand. Then the mayor spoke and told of the heroic actions of Billy and Annie and how they saved my life. They were given a wooden plaque and several gift certificates. The crowd of people began clapping again. Then people started shaking our hands and taking more pictures. Mom stood to the side, and tears flowed. They were happy tears. I couldn't help but laugh, thinking Annie and Billy may have escaped getting into too much trouble. I mean, how do you punish local heroes? I knew one thing: the three of us indeed had a lot of catching up to do. I had so many questions. I couldn't wait to get home.

Spirit Horse

Things went back to normal quickly. Mom and I didn't talk about any of this. There never seemed to be an excellent time to bring it up. I wanted to tell her more, but she wasn't asking, so I kept quiet. I tried to tell her about the people I had met and the stories they told about the Spirit Horse. But for now, I kept it to myself. Annie and Billy's family went on vacation after I came home from the hospital, so I didn't get a chance to talk to them. I wanted to know so much. Did she come in after me and couldn't find me because I was in the village? How long was I gone? What happened to me? Did I slip coming back from behind the waterfall? How did they get me off that mountain? Everything about them finding me was a blank. I didn't remember any of that. How did they get me in the canoe? I had so many questions. The doctor told my mom it was normal not to remember things after such a head injury. He said one day, I may remember, or I might not ever remember what happened.

Each day, I would walk paths around the farm and down to the creek. I would stand at the fence and leave apples. I was disappointed each day when the apples were half eaten with deer tracks around them. There were no hoofprints. I missed Blue Boy. I walked down to the creek and sat on a rock, hoping he would come. He didn't. Sometimes, I would hear the bushes move and turn only to see a squirrel or a deer coming for water. I would sit and remember the times with Blue Boy and how I loved seeing him running across the ridge. Sometimes, we would walk together side by side down to the creek. He would splash in the water like he was playing. I would get so wet. I loved it. We were a pair, he and I. Sometimes, I would sit on my rock with him beside me and tell him about my dad. I told him I was Daddy's little girl. I told him about my dad slipping me candy in church and him riding me on his shoulders. Blue Boy would listen. Sometimes I didn't speak at all. We would both enjoy the quiet. Off in the distance, we could sometimes hear coyotes howling. The water would be moving over the rocks. Occasionally, a fish would swim by. What the two of us shared was something I could never imagine. I loved Blue Boy, and I knew he loved me. I missed him every day.

I wanted to tell him that I knew he was a hero. That I knew he was the Spirit Horse. I wanted him to know how much our times together meant to me. I wanted him to know what a difference he made in my life. I wanted him to come back to me. I knew in my heart he could feel me. I knew he would come back. I would wait for as long as it took. He would come back. I knew he would.

One evening, I sat on the back porch looking at the stars. I noticed Mr. Jim had a fire going in his firepit. "Mom, I'm going to Mr. Jim's."

"Okay, honey. Tell him thanks for the collards. I'll fix him a mess tomorrow," Mom said as she was washing dishes. "Don't forget your jacket."

I rushed out the back door. Mr. Jim's house wasn't too far away. I crossed the yard, looking at his house. He kept it tidy. There were no bushes near his home, and the grass was kept short. He said he wanted to make sure he could see a snake coming. I didn't think he liked them any more than I did.

"Hi, Mr. Jim. Want some company?" I asked as I approached.

"Sure, come have a seat. How's life treating you? You look like you have recovered pretty well." He smiled as he pointed to a stump sitting near the fire. "You want some coffee? Oh, are you allowed to have coffee?" he asked.

"Thank you, but I don't like the taste. I'm good; I just finished supper. Can I talk to you about something?"

He grinned and nodded. "Sure, what do you have on your mind?"

"Mr. Jim, you've lived here a long time." He nodded again. "Have you ever heard anything about a Spirit Horse?"

He looked at me seriously and said, "I knew you would ask me about this one day. I didn't know when." I looked at him in surprise. Then he continued, "What I am going to tell you was told to me by my grandfather. It is a legend that has been passed down by the

Native Americans. He told me that there was a Native American tribe that lived on the other side of the river, not too far from here. Legend says that settlers tried to capture wild horses running free in these mountain ranges when they came here. These horses had run free for hundreds of years. The Native Americans often captured them to use them for hunting and battle if necessary. They valued these horses greatly. They were surefooted, swift, and mighty. They could go across these mountains like they had wings. Across rocks, water, and boulders, they were unstoppable. As great as these horses were, one stood above all the rest. It was said he was the most beautiful horse anyone had ever seen. His coat was black, so black it looked blue. His mane was long, and his tail trailed way behind. He was a magnificent animal with muscles that quivered even when he stood still. He carried himself as if he was king, and he was. All the other horses respected him and gave him his place of honor. Occasionally, a young stallion would challenge him. The battle between the two never lasted long, with the big stallion always standing in victory.

"The Natives were never able to capture him. Neither the young men nor the old men could outwit him. However, this horse was always there when needed. He would lead them to water if the creeks were dry. He would lead them to deer herds when food supplies were low. He would warn them of danger. He became known as the Spirit Horse. The Spirit Horse helped these people. They respected him for all he did for them. The Spirit Horse always had a large herd of mares and foals. The men of the village would capture the young colts. Spirit Horse would watch from a ridge, making sure everyone was safe. It was like he knew they needed them for their survival. To those who lived in the village, having one of his colts was a privilege. It was a sign of prosperity among the men. These people respected their horses and appreciated Spirit Horse for providing for them. They say only a select few got close to him. When seen, he was always far off. No one could say they had ever touched him because he would disappear like a ghost if they got near. But always, he would return in times of need. That is the legend I have heard about this horse." He rubbed his head as if lost in thought.

I couldn't speak at first. This legend...it was true. I finally looked at Mr. Jim and said, "I've seen him. I've seen Spirit Horse. It's Blue Boy." Mr. Jim looked up at me. I continued, "Mr. Jim, he's the one we have been looking for. You know, Blue Boy, who stayed in the pasture below us."

Mr. Jim said, "I know you've told me about a horse in the back field, and we have been looking for him, but I never saw him. I've seen you cross the field in that direction, but I can't see over the ridge."

I looked at him in anguish. "How about when you are in the garden? You can see the pasture from there, can't you?"

"Nope," he said, "never saw a horse. I saw you daily but can't say I've been in that field. The garden is on the other side of the barn; you can't see much when you head down the hill. Sorry, I can't help you. I haven't seen a horse."

"He met me at the fence every day. He would come and get treats from me. Are you sure you didn't see him?" I was concerned. "Oh, and you said the Native Americans don't live in these mountains anymore. Yes, they do: I saw them. I talked to them. They were on Buck Mountain, behind the waterfall. There were children, women, and men. They had gardens. They were skinning deer." I was pleading with him to believe me. "They told me about Blue Boy, I mean Spirit Horse. They told me he was a hero to them. The legend you just told me is true. I was there. I spoke to them." I stood up and started to cry. "Mr. Jim, please believe me. I'm not making this up. I was there."

Mr. Jim stood up and took my hand. "There are things in this world sometimes we cannot explain. This is one of them. I believe you, and I'm glad you shared this with me. You are a special lady. This may not be something I understand, but I believe you. Don't you ever let anyone tell you that what you know isn't true. You keep believing. Don't be persuaded that this is all in your head. You know in your heart you were there, and you know you have met the Spirit Horse. Keep believing." With that, he bent down, looked me straight in the eyes, and said, "I believe you."

I stayed a little longer, talking about nothing. He kept the fire going as we spoke. He was such a nice man. I was glad to have him as a friend. I knew what we discussed may have sounded crazy, but it was the truth, and he believed me. Walking home, I couldn't help but think about what I'd shared with him. The fact that he hadn't seen Blue Boy bothered me, but from where he worked, it would have been impossible to see where I used to meet him. I understood. I thought about the legend and how he had heard it from his grandfather. That had to have been a long time ago. I just wished Mr. Jim had seen Blue Boy. At least he didn't make me feel crazy. I had tried to talk to Mom at different times, but she seemed bothered when I mentioned anything about that day, so I stopped bringing it up. As I continued home, I decided to talk to Mom about seeing Blue Boy in the bottom field.

"Hi, Mom, I'm back." She was sitting in the living room working on her knitting. I asked her, "When I would go down to take apples to Blue Boy, did you ever go down there with me? I don't remember if you did or not."

She replied, "No, I never did. When hanging out clothes, I'd see you go in that direction. Sometimes, while I was washing dishes, you headed that way. I never did go down there."

I looked at her and said, "You mean you never saw Blue Boy?"

She didn't look up. "I've heard you talk about him enough, and you sure went through many apples and carrots."

I questioned again, "When you were picking wildflowers, you didn't see him? You must have. He was always at the gate waiting for me or running across the field. He would be easy for you to see."

She looked up, hearing the concern in my voice. "I never thought anything about it. I knew you were okay. My only thoughts were that you seemed to be happy, and that horse was doing something for you that I hadn't been able to do, and that was to give you peace in your life. I was happy that you were happy, and that was enough."

I was in shock. How could it be that Mom hadn't seen Blue Boy? I spent all those days with him, and she never saw him. I always ran out in the rain, and she never questioned me. She wasn't even curious about why I would stand outside in the rain to be with a horse. Wasn't she the least bit interested in seeing the horse I loved so much? I said, "I don't know what to say. You never saw him, yet you helped me look for him after he disappeared?"

"Of course I would help you. He was something you loved, and you were devastated when he went missing. Of course I'd help you look for him." Mom stopped what she was doing and questioned why I was so upset.

I was about in tears. "How could you help me look for a horse you had never seen before?"

She looked at me and said, "I figured a horse is a horse. If I found one, you would tell me whether it was him. I just did what any mother would do. Plus, I loved spending time with you. I will continue to look for him with you. We must wait till the doctor gives you clearance to go hiking. Then we will go back up to Big Sky. We could even camp overnight if you like. Wouldn't you like that?" I nodded, hugged her, said good night, and headed to my room.

I was so confused. How could it be that Mr. Jim and my mom had not seen Blue Boy at some point? How was it that I would spend time with him every day, and they never saw us together? I didn't know what to think. Was I going crazy? Did my fall in the cave make me believe all that time with Blue Boy wasn't real? Was I crazy enough to make up what I saw, the village, the people? Was it all just in my imagination? Was it real, or wasn't it? The horse I saw every day was Blue Boy, Spirit Horse. Was there even a horse at all? What about all the daily talks with him? Were they real or just something I imagined? Was I losing my mind?

Then I remembered what Mr. Jim said: hold him in your heart. Hold these memories in your heart; don't let anyone tell you it's not real. He was right. I knew I wasn't crazy. I loved Blue Boy, and he loved me. He would always be with me in my heart. I would never forget him. I would never stop looking for him because I knew he was real. I wouldn't give up. One day, he would return. He would take an apple out of my hand. He would let me lean on him and rub his beautiful coat. He would smell my hair and nuzzle my cheek. I would whisper in his ear and tell him how handsome he was and how much I loved him. One day, he would come back to me. One day, Spirit Horse would know I still needed him. He would always be in my heart. I would never give up, never. Spirit Horse, my Blue Boy, would come back.

Epilogue

It's been several months since my accident. The doctor cleared me and said I was in perfect health. I finally got to talk to Annie. She said I tried to speak as they carried me off the mountain. It was something about a ghost horse or a spirit of some kind. She said it didn't make sense. I never told her about my visit to the village or the stories they told me about the Spirit Horse. I'm glad we didn't get into too much trouble over our little excursion. But we still had to do Billy's homework. I guess that was only fair. There are days she will walk with me along the trails. She is a good friend, and I enjoy being with her so much. I don't want to talk about what I saw. I don't think she would understand, but that's okay, too.

Mom and I have started camping again on Big Sky Mountain. She is doing it for me, and I do appreciate that. I can't tell her I know where Blue Boy is. He is across the river on Buck Mountain with his herd. One day, I will go over there. I will see him again, or maybe he will see me.

Sometimes, I go to the creek and sit on a boulder by myself. I still look for him. I imagine one day, any day, he will show up. One day, I will look up, and he will be standing just over there like he used to. We will splash in the water. I will get soaked. We both will be happy again. One day, maybe today. Maybe tomorrow. He will come. The Spirit Horse, my Blue Boy, will come.

About the Author

My name is Linda Hanchey. I am in my 70's. I'm told I don't act my age. How are you supposed to act, I ask. I didn't get trained for this age, so I will continue to go the way I am. I read this quote, and it resonated with me. "Chase your dream, not perfection." That pretty much sums my life up. I have had lots of dreams. Along with that, many outstanding experiences. Let me share some of my life experiences with you.

I am a wife, a mother, a grandmother, and a great-grandmother. I have always loved horses. Born that way. I have won dance contests, been a rodeo queen, and done cowboy-mounted shooting. I've been bucked, kicked, and ridden some nice horses. My husband and I have bred, raised, and trained colts. I graduated from college in my 40s and taught in public schools for children with disabilities. In addition, opened a riding school and a handicap riding program and did that for many years. Then, in my 60s, we retired, and my husband and I moved to the mountains to ride horses in the national forests. After we moved to the mountains, at the age of 68, I went back to college to get my horse judging license. Even now, in my 70's, I judge horse events. Still looking for my next challenge and unprepared to sit in my rocking chair, I wrote my first book. As a girl growing up, we didn't have horses. My parents weren't horse people. There were no horses anywhere nearby. Books became my reality. Every book I could find, I would devour. In a book, I could ride as fast as the wind, jump as high as a mountain, and have wild adventures. It had to do until I was old enough to find them outside the books I was reading. The library never had enough books to satisfy the longing. I can remember the dreams that came with each book I read. Today, I am writing a book for that girl or boy who has this same longing and loves horses so badly that it hurts. I understand. I was that girl.

Let me leave you with this. Follow your dream no matter your age. It is worth the challenge to do something you long to do or try something new. Go for it. You may not be the best, but you will be the best version of yourself.

www.ingramcontent.com/pod-product-compliance
Lightning Source LLC
Chambersburg PA
CBHW011225120626
46545CB00010B/3162